THE PUZZLE CLUB™
MEETS THE JIGSAW KIDS

by Dandi Daley Mackall

Based on characters developed for *The Puzzle Club Christmas Mystery,* an original story by Mark Young for Lutheran Hour Ministries

Lutheran Hour
Ministries

SAINT LOUIS

Puzzle Club*™ *Mysteries
The Puzzle Club Christmas Mystery
The Puzzle Club Mystery of Great Price
The Puzzle Club Case of the Kidnapped Kid
The Puzzle Club Poison-Pen Mystery
The Puzzle Club Musical Mystery
The Puzzle Club Easter Adventure
The Puzzle Club Meets The Jigsaw Kids

Cover illustration by Mike Young Productions
Copyright © 1999 International Lutheran Laymen's League
™Trademark of International Lutheran Laymen's League

Scripture quotations taken from the HOLY BIBLE, NEW INTERNATIONAL VERSION®. NIV®. Copyright © 1973, 1978, 1984 by International Bible Society. Used by permission of Zondervan Publishing House. All rights reserved.

Published by Concordia Publishing House
3558 S. Jefferson Avenue, St. Louis, MO 63118-3968
Manufactured in the United States of America

1 2 3 4 5 6 7 8 9 10   08 07 06 05 04 03 02 01 00 99

Contents

1 Thief on the Loose!   5

2 Stop or I'll Chute!   11

3 Too Many Detectives   19

4 A Corny Case   26

5 Junkyard Jimmy's   35

6 May the Best Club *Cheat*   42
(*Cheat—Sin. Sin—Win*)
May the Best Club *Win!*

7 Getting the Picture   50

8 Unmasking the Thief   57

9 The Agony of De-Feet   64

10 Sticking Together   71

1

Thief on the Loose!

"Oh, no! Not again!"

Alex stopped his bike in front of Puzzleworks and listened. Korina rammed into his back bike tire.

"Alex!" she scolded. "Have you never heard of hand signals?"

"Shh-h-h!" Alex held his index finger to his lips and listened. The voice sounded like Tobias.

Christopher wheeled his bike to a stop beside Korina. "What's the matter?" he asked.

Clang! Crash! The banging came from the alley beside Tobias' puzzle shop.

"I think Tobias is in trouble!" Alex said.

Christopher dropped his bike and ran toward the alley. Korina and Alex stared at each other, then followed their Puzzle Club president and fearless leader into the shadowy alley.

"Tobias?" Christopher called.

Alex stopped cold at the sight of Tobias. He was holding two silver garbage can lids. Tobias looked like he was ready to play the cymbals. The two garbage cans were lying on their sides at his feet. Garbage littered the alley.

"Are you okay, Tobias?" Korina asked, running up to him.

"Yes, yes," he said, picking up the garbage cans. He stood the cans next to the building. "It's just … I don't know what a thief thinks he might find in my trash cans."

Tobias started picking up the litter in the alley—apple cores, shredded newspaper, plastic cartons, and smelly junk.

"We'll get that for you, Tobias," Christopher said.

As Korina, Christopher, and Alex policed the alley for more trash, Tobias scratched his white head and rubbed his chin. "That makes two nights in a row this has happened," Tobias said. "And that's not all. Someone broke into my puzzle shop last night."

"Tobias," Korina said, "why didn't you tell us before now?"

"I wasn't sure it was a thief until now," Tobias said. "But this is too much of a coincidence. I'm sure glad you Puzzle Club kids came along when you did."

Christopher, Korina, and Alex followed their friend inside Puzzleworks. Tobias had decorated the doorway with red and yellow cardboard leaves. They matched the real autumn leaves in the park across the street.

The minute the door opened, Alex knew something was wrong. Puzzle pieces lay scattered on the floor by the front window. Bits of trash littered the room. "A thief did this?" asked Alex.

"*Braawk! Thief!*" Sherlock, The Puzzle Club's parakeet, swooped out of the corner and landed on Alex's shoulder.

"I think Sherlock's trying to tell us something," Alex said, stroking the bird's soft green head. "Maybe Sherlock saw the thief."

"Alex," Korina said, whipping out her magnifying glass and striding toward the cash register, "do not jump to conclusions. We don't know what Sherlock saw. But we are detectives, Alex. While this certainly *looks* like the work of a thief, we must consider every possibility."

Alex hated it when Korina treated him like he didn't know how to be a detective. "*Every* possibility, Korina? Like that Tobias is a messy shopkeeper? Is that what you're saying?"

Korina didn't answer him. Alex pulled out his detective's notebook and began recording clues.

Near the door an alphabet puzzle had been shoved off of a display shelf. Alex tried to see if any of the pieces were missing. He had helped Tobias put that particular puzzle together—it was about food. Alex looked for the *A = Apple* piece, but he couldn't find it. He jotted the clue in his notebook.

"This is how the intruder got in," Korina announced. She was examining a fallen screen under the west window. "The person must have popped the screen out."

Korina stood up and peered through her magnifying glass at a yellow leaf that she held in her hand. "Hmmm," she said, turning the leaf over. "The intruder must have dragged this in with him—or her." She glanced at Alex. "Note how I resist the urge to jump to conclusions."

Christopher rushed over with his camera and snapped a shot of the leaf. "It's hard to tell what's missing," he said. "Let's help Tobias straighten up this place. Then maybe we can see what this person was after."

The biggest mess was behind Tobias' counter. "Wait!" Alex said as Korina grabbed a handful of candy wrappers from the floor. "I need to write down what's there before you destroy the evidence, Korina."

Korina gave Alex one of her looks, but she stopped and studied the wrappers. "What is all this, Tobias?" she asked.

Tobias' face reddened. "I ... well ... I keep a few snacks hidden behind my counter. Maybe the thief did me a favor. I shouldn't eat candy." Tobias chuckled.

"Maybe the intruder was hungry," Christopher said. "The only thing we've found missing is food."

"And pictures of food," Alex added, remembering the food alphabet puzzle.

"*Braawk! Braawk!*" Sherlock darted toward the fake wall of shelves that hid the secret entrance to Puzzle Club headquarters. Then he dive-bombed Alex.

"Hey! Stop it, Sherlock!" Alex yelled, ducking. "I didn't do anything."

"Sherlock's trying to tell us something," Christopher said.

Sherlock flew to Tobias, then he soared behind the counter. When he flew out, he held a gold string in his beak. It was a piece of the gold cord Tobias pulled to let the kids into the secret Puzzle Club headquarters.

"That's it!" Christopher said. "Sherlock's trying to tell us to go up to headquarters. Pull the cord, Tobias!"

Tobias reached behind the counter and pulled the gold cord. The shelves on the side of the wall slid to the side to reveal an arched entrance. Alex beat Korina to the secret stairway. He thundered up the stairs and turned the doorknob just as Korina yelled, "Alex, punch in the code!"

But it was too late. The Puzzle Club security system activated. Sirens wailed and whistles blew. Korina reached past Alex to punch in the security code.

Alex peered inside headquarters. What he saw froze him in his tracks. Hats, scarves, wigs, and pieces of costumes lay scattered across the floor. When the sirens shut off, Alex heard another noise. *Scrape, shoooosh, scrape.*

He turned in the direction of the noise—toward the secret Puzzle Club slide. Alex looked up just in time to see The Puzzle Club logo—the big private eye symbol—open. Then someone—or something—passed in front of the opening. It was too dark to see anything except a moving shadow as it disappeared down the slide.

"Quick!" Alex screamed. "The thief is getting away!"

2

Stop or I'll Chute!

"After him!" Alex shouted. He lunged toward the chute, but he forgot he was still standing on the stairs. Alex tripped on the top step and fell face down inside headquarters.

"Step aside, Alex," Korina said, hopping over him as he lay sprawled on the floor. "I'll get that thief!"

"Are you okay?" Christopher asked as he ran by.

"Sure," Alex said, scraping himself off the floor. "Never felt better." Sherlock whizzed by overhead. Alex plopped back down on his stomach. "Thanks a lot, Sherlock," he muttered.

Inches from his nose, Alex's yellow miner's hard hat was spinning upside down. He grabbed the hat, clicked on the light, and stuck the hat on his head. A beam of light shone from Alex's hat into headquarters. The place was a mess! But he couldn't worry about that now. He didn't want to miss out on the capture. "Wait for me!"

Alex struggled to his feet just in time to see Korina and Christopher approach the secret chute. The big eye opened, and Korina, then Christopher, climbed inside.

"Stop in the name of The Puzzle Club!" shouted Korina as she pushed off and disappeared. Her voice echoed as she banged down the metal slide.

"I'm right behind you!" yelled Christopher. His brown hair vanished down the black hole of the chute.

By the time Alex reached the private eye logo, the big eye had closed. He had to push it open again. "Here I come, ready or not!" He jumped to the top of the chute and braced himself for the long, winding slide down. The beam of light from his miner's hat pierced the dark passage ahead of him.

Alex wound down and around, picking up speed, hanging onto his hat with one hand. When he got to the middle of the chute, it divided into different passages. One led to the street out front. One took him back to Puzzleworks. Another emptied into the alley.

Alex figured Christopher and Korina hadn't gone back to Puzzleworks. He thought he heard voices at the end of the street passage. Alex guided himself toward the street tunnel. But before he turned the corner, he flashed his helmet light down the alley tunnel.

"Ahh-hh-hh!" Alex screamed until he ran out of air. Staring back at him from the tunnel were two horrible, red, beady eyes shining from a masked face!

Alex pushed off in the opposite direction. He thought his feet would never reach the street. Finally, he slid out of the secret chute and landed right in front of Korina.

"Alex, what is the meaning of screaming like that? Do you want to scare off the thief?" Korina asked.

"I saw it!" Alex said. "A horrible monster! It almost got me! If I hadn't been quick, I think it might have eaten me! It had red eyes that burned like fire! And it wore a mask!"

"Alex, Alex," Korina said as if she were scolding a little kid. "How many times do we have to tell you not to jump to conclusions?"

Christopher ran to the chute and peered inside. "I don't see anything," he said, his voice echoing in the tunnel. He stuck his camera inside and clicked it. "I'll develop these later and see if my camera picked up any clues. Let's check with Tobias. Maybe the thief took the chute back into Puzzleworks."

They ran back inside Tobias' puzzle shop. Tobias was wrapping a puzzle for a customer. Alex recognized the stout figure of Mrs. O'Grady, one of Tobias' regular customers.

"Tobias," Christopher said, "did you see anyone run in here?"

"No, I didn't," said Tobias. With a big smile, he handed Mrs. O'Grady her puzzle. It was no wonder people liked to buy from Tobias. Alex figured Tobias was the kindest person in New Bristol—maybe in the whole world. Already Alex's knees had stopped knocking and his heartbeat felt slower.

"I guess our thief made a successful escape, thanks to Alex," said Korina.

"Thief?" asked Mrs. O'Grady. "Why, I told Miss Jones this morning that I thought we'd had a thief at the church."

"Did you report this to the sheriff?" asked Korina.

"No, I didn't," said Mrs. O'Grady. "The only thing missing was a bag of nuts. We're having our annual sale to help the animal shelter, you know. Well, Miss Jones suggested maybe one of the other women ate the nuts. I didn't want to embarrass anybody. Do you suppose it really was your thief?"

A picture of those glowing red eyes flashed through Alex's mind. That red-eyed monster had even stolen from the church! Alex thought back to other Puzzle Club cases with ghosts—the musical mystery, the Christmas mystery. Of course, The Puzzle Club had found out that there weren't really any ghosts. But he'd never seen anything like this red-eyed, masked bandit. Mrs. O'Grady should be thankful that she hadn't seen the horrible monster!

"Christopher," said Tobias, "maybe it's time you went to Sheriff Grimaldi."

"I'm sure the sheriff will be glad to know The Puzzle Club is on the case!" said Mrs. O'Grady.

As The Puzzle Club biked toward the sheriff's office, leaves crunched under their wheels. Mr. Rafferty, the park maintenance man, stopped raking leaves to wave at Christopher, Korina, and Alex. Sherlock clung to Alex's handlebars. Alex made sure he didn't fall behind. He felt as if those scary red eyes were watching every move he made.

The kids pulled their bikes onto the curb in front of the sheriff's office. "We'd better lock our bikes," Christopher said, leading the way to the bike rack.

Three bikes hogged most of the rack so The Puzzle Club could barely squeeze their bikes in. Alex parked next to a red version of his blue 10-speed bike. "Hmm," he said. "This doesn't look like Patrick's." Patrick Grimaldi, the sheriff's son, often visited his dad at work, parking a more expensive version of Alex's bike out front.

"I haven't seen this silver bike before either," Korina said. She eyed the weird metal box on the handlebars. Wires came out of the box and ran every which way. Korina examined the gizmo through her magnifying glass. "It looks like a type of wind meter," she said.

"Come on, Korina," Christopher said, edging his bike in next to a girl's bike about the same size as his. "Sheriff!" Christopher called, leading the way inside the office.

Christopher stopped. Sheriff Grimaldi poked his head out from a group of kids Alex had never seen before. There were three of them—two girls and a boy. And they seemed to be deep in conversation with the sheriff.

"Oops," Christopher said, "sorry. I didn't know you ... uh ... had company. We're here on official business, Sheriff—if we could talk to you ... in private. We'll be glad to wait until you finish with your ... friends, of course."

A tall, thin girl with long, blonde hair turned and spoke. "Excuse us, please. We're in the middle of official police business. Could you kids come back later?"

"Kids?" Korina asked, her voice rising. We are here on detective business. We really don't have time to waste."

"Detective business?" asked a boy. Alex couldn't believe how much he looked like a male version of Korina. He even had a magnifying glass in his hand! And it looked bigger than Korina's! "*We* are here on detective business," he said.

"You?" Alex said. "But *we're* the detectives around here. We're The Puzzle Club."

A girl at least a year younger than Alex stared up at him. "Maybe one of these three is the thief," she said, narrowing her eyes at Alex. "They look like they might be up to something, don't you think? Such a shame since one of them is so handsome." She batted her long eyelashes at Alex.

"Amanda," said the boy with the magnifying glass, "will you stop jumping to conclusions?"

"Wait a minute," Christopher said. "Let's start over here. I'm Christopher. This is Korina. And this is Alex. We're The Puzzle Club detectives."

The blonde girl stepped forward and shook Christopher's hand. She was probably 14, like

Christopher, and stood an inch or two shorter than him. "I'm Flash," she said. "Pleased to meet you." Now Alex could see her camera. It looked like the kind that developed pictures instantly. Patrick had one just like it.

Flash pointed to the boy. He was busy examining Korina's shoes through his magnifying glass. "This is Kirk," Flash said, pulling him up by his collar. "And that's Amanda. We're The Jigsaw Kids. We're visiting Amanda's grandfather."

"And I would say," said Kirk, "that it is rather a good thing for New Bristol that we are vacationing here. We have—how shall I say this without sounding like I'm bragging?—a reputation."

"Um, that's good," Christopher said. He turned to the sheriff. "Sheriff, we're here because someone broke into Puzzleworks. And Mrs. O'Grady thinks someone stole a bag of nuts from church. Now, as far as we know, nothing serious has been taken—yet. But—"

"You don't have to worry anymore," said Flash. "Really—Christopher, is it? Really, Christopher, it should be safe for you kids to go home now. As we've just been telling Sheriff Grimaldi, we are pretty famous for solving mysteries where we come from. So don't worry—The Jigsaw Kids are on the case!"

3

Too Many Detectives

Amanda pulled out a pink spiral notebook and a huge red pen. Her notebook looked a lot like Alex's blue one, except his had lines. Amanda stared Alex up and down. "Alex," she said, "before you go, I have a few questions for you. Did I hear someone say this Mrs. O'Grady complained of a theft?"

Alex didn't want all his detective work to end up as a red note in some girl's stupid pink notebook. He glanced at Christopher, but Christopher smiled and nodded for him to answer. "Yes," Alex said, not looking at Amanda.

Amanda scribbled something that looked 10 times as long as *yes*. "And you claim that a puzzle shop was broken into? And someone stole puzzles?" she asked.

Again Alex looked to Christopher to get him out of this. This time Christopher answered. "Yes,

Puzzleworks, our friend Tobias' shop, appears to have been broken into," said the Puzzle Club leader. "But it looks like all the intruder took were candy bars, some gum, and maybe a couple of puzzle pieces."

Instead of writing in her notebook, Amanda stepped closer to Alex. "Where were you this morning between the hours of 6 and 7 A.M.?"

"That does it!" Alex said. He whipped out his own notebook. "Where were you?" Amanda and Alex stood nose to nose, notebook to notebook, until Christopher broke them up.

"Alex, where are your manners?" Christopher asked. "The Jigsaw Kids are visiting our town." He turned to Flash. "I think it's great you're already trying to help. In fact, if you don't mind, I'd like to take your picture." Christopher raised his camera, stepped backward, and snapped the shutter.

Flash! At the same instant that Christopher's flash went off, an even bigger light burst from Flash's camera. Out came a picture instantly. "Hope you don't mind," Flash said, glancing at her watch. "It's just for the record," she explained, waving the perfect photograph she'd just taken of The Puzzle Club.

"Wow," Christopher said, looking at the photo. "Hope mine comes out this good. It will take me a couple of hours to develop it."

"Well and good," Kirk said. "But perhaps we should get our plan underway for trapping the criminal with my Kirk-o-dex."

"Your what-o-dex?" Korina asked, frowning at Kirk the way she frowned at Alex when he said something stupid.

"In layman's—or laywoman's—terms, you might think of the Kirk-o-dex as a lie detector to catch the thief in his own lies." Kirk pulled out from behind his back something that looked like a Ping-Pong paddle. "I'd explain, but it is rather complex."

Alex watched Korina's face turn red as she took a deep breath. "Complex? I'll show you—"

Christopher moved between Korina and Kirk. "Uh, Korina," he said. "Don't we have official Puzzle Club business to take care of?"

Sheriff Grimaldi slammed something down on his desk. The noise made everybody turn toward the sheriff. "See this poster?" he asked.

"I brought him that," Amanda whispered to Alex. It read: *Church Crafts and Bake Sale, Saturday. All profits will go to the New Bristol Animal Shelter.*

"I think you know that the animal shelter counts on the church's annual sale to keep it operating," said Sheriff Grimaldi. "I don't have to tell you what will happen to those animals if the shelter can't afford to house and feed them."

"Excuse me, Sheriff," Christopher said, "but what does the church sale have to do with these little thefts?"

"Let me explain," said Flash. "You apparently aren't aware that nuts weren't the only thing taken from the church. A few other thefts, like your friend's puzzle pieces, may or may not be related to the *real* case—the church thefts."

"I knew about the thefts first," said Amanda. "My grandfather cleans the building, and he discovered the break-in. He told me about it."

"The church sale is on Saturday," said Sheriff Grimaldi. "Maybe between The Puzzle Club and The Jigsaw Kids, we can solve the mystery in time."

"But—" Korina and Alex, Kirk and Amanda started to protest.

"The sheriff is right," said Christopher. "It sounds like you Jigsaw Kids are on to something. How can we help?"

Christopher and Flash worked out a plan while Alex and Amanda stared each other down. Finally Alex blinked.

"You're kind of cute when you stare," Amanda said. She twirled her long black braid around her finger and grinned at Alex. It made him nervous.

"Flash," Kirk called, "I'm going to check my trail."

"Your trail?" Korina asked.

Flash explained. "That's Kirk Code for *bike*. Trail—hike. Hike—bike. The first pair of words are similar. The next two words rhyme. He's going out to check his bike."

Kirk gave Flash a dirty look, probably for revealing his silly code. Then Korina followed Kirk outside to look at the *kirk-o-meter* he'd made for his bike.

"Let's split up into teams," Christopher said. "Jigsaw Kids can fill us in on the details of the church thefts. And we can show them around New Bristol."

"But we're already a team," Alex protested. "Why can't The Puzzle Club solve this case by ourselves like we've solved every other case?"

"Come on, Alex," Christopher said. "It'll be fun."

Korina and Kirk walked back into the office. Looking at the two of them, Alex figured they weren't having fun either.

"I still say you will not experience accuracy unless you allow for the velocity of your bike," Korina said.

"Are you suggesting that I have not thought of the velocity of my bike?" Kirk demanded. "Diamonds!"

Amanda whispered to Alex. "*Diamonds—pearls. Pearls—Girls!* Kirk Code is pretty easy once you get the hang of it."

Christopher cleared his throat. "Korina? Kirk? Flash and I have a plan of action for this case. Before we go any farther, though, I'd like The Jigsaw Kids to meet Tobias."

Kirk and Amanda groaned. Alex felt like groaning too. Why couldn't the great Jigsaw Kids get their own Tobias? The Puzzle Club was fine just like it was: Tobias, Christopher, Korina, Alex, and Sherlock.

Sherlock! Where was that bird? What if Red-Eyes had captured poor Sherlock? Alex put his pinkie and index fingers to his lips and whistled the Puzzle Club whistle.

Still no Sherlock. Something moved on Sheriff Grimaldi's desk. Alex watched in horror as the sheriff's hat jumped to the left, then to the right. "It's the ghost thief!" Alex cried.

"Stand back!" shouted Amanda, grabbing a broom from the corner of the office. She stood in front of the desk and swung the broom back over her shoulder. She looked like she was standing over home plate, waiting for the right pitch.

"*Braawk! Braawk!*" screeched the hat. Sherlock flew out from under the sheriff's hat and dived at Amanda. She screamed and ducked.

24

"Sherlock!" Alex called.

"Sherlock?" Amanda repeated.

"*Braawk! Sherlock!*" said the Puzzle Club mascot, coming to rest on Christopher's shoulder.

"*SQUAWK! SHERLOCK!*" wailed a loud, eerie voice that definitely wasn't Sherlock's. It came from somewhere behind Alex. But before he could turn around, something heavy landed on his head.

Alex froze. He felt huge claws dig into his hair. He imagined those red, glowing eyes and thought he might faint.

Amanda dropped her broom and burst into giggles. Kirk and Flash laughed too. Then even Korina and Christopher were laughing. Laughing! And all the while, Alex felt the horrible monster sitting on top of his head. Why had he taken off his miner's helmet? Why was everyone laughing?

"Hey!" Alex shouted. "What's the matter with everybody? Help me! Will somebody tell me what's going on?"

"*SQUAWK! ELEMENTARY! SQUAWK!*" said the monster on Alex's head.

Amanda stepped in front of Alex and held out her arm. A huge parrot flew from Alex's head to roost on Amanda's arm. "This," she said, stroking the green feathered beast, "is the Jigsaw Kids' mascot. I'd like you to meet dear Watson."

4

A Corny Case

"*SQUAWK! ELEMENTARY, DEAR WATSON!*" said the parrot.

"He's great!" Christopher said, leaning on the desk next to Amanda. "Sherlock, meet Watson."

Sherlock drew himself up to his full height and fluffed out his feathers. He stretched his neck toward Watson and cocked his head to the side. "*Braawk! Sherlock!*" he screeched.

"*SQUAWK! WATSON!*" replied the parrot.

Poor Sherlock took off, flew around the office, and wiggled back under the sheriff's hat.

"Well," Flash said, sounding to Alex as if she thought she were in charge, "it's time to get to work. Christopher and I will go straight to the church and conduct interviews. Kirk, you and Korina look around town for clues."

"Uh ... okay, Flash," Christopher said. "I kind of wanted you guys to meet Tobias, but I guess we can do that later. We can meet at Puzzleworks when we're done."

Flash checked her watch. "Everyone report to Puzzleworks at 1700 hours. That's 5 P.M. civilian time." She raised her camera and snapped a picture of the startled sheriff. Then she turned to leave.

"Wait!" Alex said. "What about me? Where should I start?"

"Yeah, what about me?" Amanda asked. Then she gave Alex a huge smile. "Me and Alex."

Flash shrugged. Kirk said, "Just try not to get into trouble. We do not want to waste time getting you out of trouble."

"Oh, is that so?" Amanda said. She picked up the broom again and glared at Kirk.

"Maybe Alex and Amanda could nose around the church too," Christopher said. "Alex, take notes on everything."

Alex pulled out his notebook. "I'll write down any clues I find." He pretended to write something important.

"Me too!" Amanda said, pulling out her pink notebook. Alex watched as Amanda scribbled on a blank sheet: *Amanda + Alex.*

Oh, brother! Alex thought. *Why did they stick me with this kid?*

"The game is afoot!" declared Kirk. Before the others could reach the door, Kirk pulled something that looked like a squirt gun out of his pocket. He aimed it at the door to the sheriff's office. A big round, flat piece of metal shot out and stuck like a magnet to the doorknob. With a flick of his wrist, Kirk yanked the door open.

"How did you do that?" asked Sheriff Grimaldi.

"*SQUAWK! ELEMENTARY!*" said Watson as The Jigsaw Kids and The Puzzle Club left the office.

Flash and Christopher hopped on their bikes and headed in one direction. Watson and Sherlock perched on their handlebars. Korina and Kirk left in the opposite direction. Alex tried to catch up with Christopher, but no matter how fast he pedaled, he couldn't shake Amanda. Her pink bike stayed wheel to wheel with his.

Amanda smiled at him as they biked toward the east end of New Bristol. "I'll bet a handsome boy like you has a lot of girlfriends, huh?" she asked.

Alex groaned and tried to pretend he hadn't heard her. Okay. So what if Amanda had pretty hair and boys like Patrick Grimaldi would probably call her cute. As far as Alex was concerned, girls were a complete mystery! He just didn't understand them.

"Just look for clues," Alex said, careful not to look at Amanda. "Let me know if you see the slightest thing. It may not mean anything to you, but for me, it could be the clue that solves the mystery."

Alex glanced at Amanda. She was riding her bike without holding on to the handlebars. Then she actually took out her notebook and wrote something down—without falling behind.

The church's grassy, tree-filled lot might have been the prettiest spot in New Bristol, if it hadn't been sitting next to a junkyard. Through the church's windows, parishioners stared out at wrecked cars, rusted trailers, and piles of junk.

Alex and Amanda braked to a stop next to Christopher and Flash. "What's that smell?" Amanda asked, turning up her already turned-up nose.

"It's coming from the junkyard," Alex said. He sniffed the air. "Smells like burnt rubber." To tell the truth, Alex kind of liked the junkyard. That was where he'd found the parts for his super crook-grabber, the invention that had helped The Puzzle Club during their Easter adventure.

A tall, burly man was mowing grass behind the church. "That's my grandfather," Amanda said, waving to the man. "He's the custodian here. If it hadn't been for Grandpa, we might never have stumbled on to this case."

Amanda led the way into the church basement. Long metal tables were set up on the cement floor at one end of the basement. Half a dozen women scurried between the kitchen and the tables.

"Alex!" It was Miss Jones, one of Alex's old Sunday school teachers and his former kindergarten teacher. She motioned for him to join her behind one of the silver tables. She was setting out wreaths made from vines. "I am so relieved The Puzzle Club is on the case!" she said.

Alex couldn't resist a proud grin in Amanda's direction.

"And who might this young lady be, Alex?" asked Miss Jones.

Before Alex could answer, Amanda stepped in front of him and shook Miss Jones' hand. "I'm Amanda," she said. "I'm one of the Jigsaw Kid detectives. We're here to solve the mystery." She took out her pink notebook. "Please tell me everything you know, ma'am."

Miss Jones looked confused, but she answered Amanda's question. "This morning when I got here, Millie came running up in a tizzy. Someone had raided the box of Indian corn for our centerpieces. Ears of corn had been stripped of kernels," Miss Jones explained.

Alex wrote everything down in his notebook. Even though he had lines and Amanda didn't, her writing looked a hundred times neater than his. "Was anything else taken?" he asked.

"I don't think so," Miss Jones replied, "but things were quite disturbed. The custodian said he found boxes overturned when he came in to clean last night. I guess it was worse before he cleaned up. Who would do such a thing, Alex?" But before he could answer, Miss Jones hurried off to meet Mrs. Willakers, who was just coming down the stairs.

When Alex looked up from his notebook, he saw Amanda staring at him. "I think we make a great team, don't you, Alex?" she asked.

Alex ignored the question and looked around for Christopher. Suddenly a scream came through the window not three feet from Alex. Alex spotted Christopher and Flash at the far end of the basement. He turned and raced up the stairs only to find that Amanda had beaten him to the top.

The scream came again. Alex and Amanda raced toward the sound. Outside the basement entrance stood little Meg Willakers. She was crying, her face hidden in her hands. Alex knelt beside her. "Meggie," he said, "are you okay?"

Meg shook her head no and let out another wail. The sun had gone behind the clouds while Alex and Amanda were inside. Now it seemed dark outside, almost like night.

"Come on, Alex," Amanda said. "There's no thief here."

Christopher and Flash ran up. "What's the matter?" asked Christopher. "Meg, are you all right?" He knelt on the other side of her. She stopped sobbing.

"Christopher," said Flash, "we're wasting valuable time."

Christopher looked into Meg's face. "Meg," he said softly, "why did you scream? Did you see something?"

Meg nodded yes. Amanda sighed deeply, and Flash shifted her weight from one foot to the other.

Christopher went on in the same gentle voice. "What did you see? Can you tell us?"

"It was scary!" Meg said. "Like a monster!"

"*Now* can we get back to our investigation?" Flash asked.

Christopher acted as though he hadn't heard Flash. "Meg, tell me exactly what you saw, or thought you saw."

"I didn't get a good look," she said, sniffing. "Grandma sent me back to the car for this." She held up a sack of bright orange yarn.

"Christopher?" Flash said in a sharp voice.

"That's nice of you, Meg," Christopher said. "Go on. What did you see?"

"I heard leaves rustling behind the church. I thought Grandma might be there. Then something ran toward the junkyard," Meg said. She started crying again.

"Something, Meg, or someone?" Christopher asked.

"I don't know," she said, her voice shaking. "I got scared and closed my eyes. Then I-I-I screamed."

"I can't waste any more time with this," said Flash. "Amanda, we need to get out of here. Christopher, we'll meet you at 1700 hours at that puzzle shop. The Jigsaw Kids have a case to solve." Flash marched off, tugging Amanda along behind her.

"Okay, Flash," Christopher called after them. "See you then." He turned back to Meg. "Will you show us where you first saw ... or heard ... whatever it was?"

Meg shook her head fast. "I'm scared!" she said.

"We'll be right here with you, Meg," Christopher said.

Meg tiptoed toward the back of the church, stopping twice on the way to grab hold of Christopher's hand. Alex wondered if maybe Meg was making the whole thing up just to get Christopher's attention. Then Meg stopped and pointed at the ground in front of a basement window, refusing to go any closer.

Christopher turned to Meg, who stood back and covered her face. "Meg, why don't you go find your grandma? You've been a big help. Thanks for being so brave," he said.

Meg smiled so big that Alex could see she had four teeth missing. Then she ran into the church, hollering for her granny.

Alex followed Christopher to the ground-level window. They felt all around on the ground. Alex poked under the fallen leaves. He felt something. He picked up a handful of small, hard, colorful things. They looked like purple and orange teeth!

5

Junkyard Jimmy's

"Christopher!" Alex yelled. "The monster … red eyes … purple teeth!"

Christopher fingered the tooth-shaped pieces in Alex's hand. "Good job, Alex!" he said. "A clue. This looks like Indian corn."

Indian corn? Not monster teeth? "Uh … sure, Christopher," Alex said, trying to act calm. "Indian corn. That's what I thought."

Christopher and Alex filled their pockets with the colorful kernels. "This may turn out to be evidence," Christopher said. "Meg said she saw something or someone run into Junkyard Jimmy's. We had better check it out."

Alex and Christopher crossed the churchyard and ducked under a wire fence. Alex stood for a minute and looked at the pile of junk in Junkyard Jimmy's. It made him think of a metal ocean.

Rusted car parts were scattered around the sea of metal like wrecked boats.

A horn honked, and Alex jumped a mile into the air. He turned toward the sound, but he couldn't see anybody in any of the wrecked cars.

"I think it came from that red Volkswagen," Christopher said.

The kids walked over and peeked through a broken window. The bug-shaped car was missing two wheels, a backseat, and the radio. One fuzzy lime-green dice—or was it *die*?—dangled from the rearview mirror. Alex wouldn't mind owning a car like this himself—only not a broken one.

"Kind," Alex said, trying out Kirk Code. "Get it? *Kind—nice. Nice—dice.* Get it, Christopher? You just—"

Alex stopped. He heard footsteps coming up fast from behind. Before he could turn around, something pounced against his back. Alex fell forward onto gravel. "Help!" he cried.

Something was standing on his back, pushing him into the hard, scraping gravel. Alex used all of his might to turn over onto his back and face his attacker. A huge black-and-tan dog stood on top of Alex, his big paws planted on Alex's stomach.

Alex started to holler, but the dog leaned its head down into Alex's face. Alex closed his eyes. Then he felt something rough and wet on his cheek. The dog was licking him!

"Here, fellow! Here, Hamlet!" Junkyard Jimmy was calling his dog. "I fear my canine once again proves inadequate as a watchdog. Come, Hamlet."

The dog leapt off Alex and raced to his master. He jumped up on Jimmy and licked his face.

"Yes, my fair one," Jimmy cooed.

Alex stood up and brushed himself off. Junkyard Jimmy was dressed in gray from his gray baseball cap to his gray boots. He was thin, and his skin looked like leather. His eyes were tiny, the kind people called beady. You would never guess that he'd let a dog lick his face.

"In truth," Junkyard Jimmy said, squinting at Christopher, "are you not the renowned Puzzle Club children? Hamlet and I are honored. Might we find ourselves in the midst of a mystery?" The whole time he talked, he continued petting his dog.

Christopher shook Jimmy's free hand. "I'm Christopher, and this is Alex," he said. "We are on a case, but we don't know yet if you're involved in it. Someone said they might have seen a thief run into your junkyard within the last hour. Did you see anything suspicious?"

"Here? Suspicious?" Junkyard Jimmy took off his cap and wiped at the red line it left on his completely bald head. "Nary a suspect. Perhaps the individual merely saw Hamlet here."

Alex took the disappointment hard, like a blow to his chest. He wanted to solve the mystery and show Amanda and The Jigsaw Kids who the real detectives were. "I guess Flash and Amanda were right," Alex said.

Junkyard Jimmy left to get Hamlet a hamburger. Christopher walked back toward the red Volkswagen and snapped a few pictures of the outside and the inside of the car. Alex didn't understand why he wanted to waste more film and more time.

As Christopher and Alex biked to Puzzleworks for the meeting, the sky grew even darker, and it looked like rain. Alex tried to think of a nice way to say what was on his mind. "Christopher," Alex finally said, "I don't … I don't like working with The Jigsaw Kids. I liked it better when it was just us."

Christopher didn't answer right away. Then he said, "Alex, I know how you feel. But Flash, Kirk, and Amanda probably haven't made many friends here. Besides, making new friends does not mean you give up your old friends. You know what Tobias always says about how Jesus is our best friend and He will help us be friends with other people. If that means investigating this mystery with The Jigsaw Kids, then we can make room. Right?"

Alex didn't really have an answer. "Christopher," he said, changing the subject, "where's Sherlock?" Alex couldn't remember seeing their mascot since Meg Willakers had screamed.

"I'm afraid poor Sherlock agreed with you about The Jigsaw Kids," said Christopher. "He didn't seem to like Watson very much."

Christopher and Alex parked their bikes outside Puzzleworks and went inside. Alex was relieved to find Tobias alone. "Hi, Tobias," he called.

Sherlock flew over for a greeting. "*Braawk! Hi!*" said the parakeet, landing on Alex's shoulder.

"Hi, Alex. Hello, Christopher," Tobias said. He brought out glasses of lemonade. Alex downed his in one gulp.

"Sheriff Grimaldi called," said Tobias, refilling Alex's glass. "He said you've got some help with this case."

"Hmmf," Alex muttered.

"He told me all about The Jigsaw Kids," Tobias continued. "I think it's wonderful that you kids have found some new friends. You should get this mystery solved in record time. Good thing too. The word around town is that the craft and bake sale is in trouble. That means the animal shelter is in trouble too."

The door burst open and Korina and Kirk stormed in. "Oh, yes?" shouted Korina. "You obviously do not have a grasp of science!" She folded her arms and turned her back on Kirk.

"A lot you know, Miss Unscientific Inventor!" Kirk responded. "Your thief-trapper is ... is ... mushy!"

Alex decoded in his head. *Mushy—Cupid. Cupid—Stupid.* He hoped Korina wasn't on to Kirk Code yet.

Korina wheeled on Kirk just as Flash and Amanda strolled into the puzzle shop. "You and your fellow Jigsaw Kids are absolutely juvenile! We do not need you on this case," Korina said. "In fact, I wish the three of you would just—as Kirk would say—*Stitch wander!*"

Flash, Amanda, and Kirk must have decoded Korina's words instantly. Without a word, the three of them headed for the door.

"Wait!" Christopher hollered. "We want you on the case with us!"

Flash turned, her nose in the air, her chin held high. "Thank you very much, but we *are* on the case. Just not with you. Go ahead and try to solve it, Puzzle Club. Just don't get in our way. The Jigsaw Kids are about to show all of New Bristol who the real detectives are." With that, she spun on her heel and marched out the door.

Kirk did exactly the same heel spin and followed Flash out the door. Amanda trailed behind. Before the door slammed after her, she turned a sad face toward Alex and mouthed the words, *Bye, Alex.*

Alex was still frowning in concentration, trying to decode what Korina had said. *Stitch wander. Stitch wander.* Finally he cracked it: *Stitch— Sew. Sew—Go. Wander—roam. Roam—home.*

"I got it!" Alex shouted. "Jigsaw Kids, *go home!*"

6

May the Best Club *Cheat* (*Cheat—Sin. Sin—Win*) May the Best Club *Win!*

Alex stared at the door to Puzzleworks, which was still shaking on its hinges.

"Korina, why did you do that?" Christopher asked.

"Those poor children," said Tobias. "Now they don't even have The Puzzle Club for friends."

"They're not poor!" Korina said. But she had a pained look on her face. "You should have heard the things Kirk said to me."

Tobias walked over and hugged Korina. Alex knew from experience that a hug from Tobias could make you feel great. Or it could make you feel guilty. Korina looked like guilt was breaking through her anger. She wiped at the tears that started down her cheeks. Alex didn't think he'd ever seen her cry.

"I'm sorry, Tobias," Korina said. "That boy just makes me so mad. I know we should try to be their friends, but it's just so hard with Kirk."

Tobias held Korina at arm's length with a hand on each shoulder. He gave her his warmest Tobias smile. "Korina, if it were easy, you would not need God to help you, would you? Why don't you talk to Him about it?" Tobias suggested. "You'd be surprised how much Jesus knows about friendship."

"But, Tobias," Korina said, "Kirk is more like an enemy than a friend!" She'd stopped crying and was staring up at Tobias.

"Remember what Jesus said about loving our enemies?" Tobias asked. " 'Love your enemies and pray for those who persecute you. ... For if you love those who love you, what reward will you get?' And Jesus loved His enemies enough to die for them—for us—on the cross."

"Tobias is right, Korina," Christopher said. "It's easy to love the friends who love us. But God can help us love when it's not so easy."

Korina grinned. "It is unfortunate that I cannot invent a scientific transformer to turn enemies into friends—or Kirks into frogs." Korina laughed. "I am only joking. Even scientists jest on occasion. I shall ask Jesus to help me model friendship for Kirk."

Alex was thinking of Amanda. Maybe he should give her another chance. She wasn't *that* bad. If Jesus could love His enemies, Alex figured he could be friendly to an annoying girl.

Sherlock, still perched on Alex's shoulder, flapped his wings. Alex tried to turn his head to face the bird. "What do you say, Sherlock?" he asked. "Shall we give friendship a try? Are you ready to make friends with Watson?"

"*Braawk! Watson! Braawk! Friend!*" said Sherlock.

"Good," Christopher said. "Then it's agreed. Let's go find—"

Miss Jones burst into the store. "Puzzle Club!" she said, "I'm so glad I found you!"

"What's wrong, Miss Jones?" Alex asked, running to meet his old teacher.

Miss Jones panted to catch her breath. "Church ... nuts ... flour ... raisins ... gone!"

"More thefts?" Christopher asked, helping Miss Jones to the overstuffed couch in the puzzle corner.

"Yes! And the other ladies are threatening to quit!" said Miss Jones. "They're all frightened the thief will come while they're baking cookies and pies. It's a disaster! You have to come right now and see for yourselves."

Christopher looked at Tobias. "Go with Miss Jones," Tobias said. "I'll see if I can find Kirk and the others and make things right. You can talk to them when you get back. Hurry!"

Miss Jones drove The Puzzle Club to the church in her battered brown station wagon. They arrived in time to see three ladies running to their cars. Christopher hopped out of the car and tried to talk to the women, but they refused to stop. Alex and Korina stood outside Miss Jones' car, waiting for Christopher.

"Uh ... Alex?" Miss Jones called through the car window. "Tell Christopher and Korina I'll wait for you children in the car." Then she rolled the window up.

Christopher motioned for Alex and Korina to follow him. Inside the church, a quick investigation of the kitchen turned up the following clues, which Alex duly noted in his notebook:

> Flour and sugar bags torn open
> Flour and sugar all over floor
> 3 raisins on floor; 1 empty raisin box
> Empty bag of nuts
> Main suspect: Hungry Ghost Thief!

"Move, Alex," Korina said. "I need to make footprint molds and dust for fingerprints, though I fear too many cooks have spoiled the prints." She crawled around, staring through her magnifying glass at the piles of white on the kitchen floor.

Alex moved to the main basement room. The first thing he noticed was a trail of bright orange yarn. It ran up one table and down another, twisted across the floor, and snaked under a rug. That ghost thief theory was starting to sound better and better. Alex glanced around the basement. Maybe Amanda was on the job somewhere. But he didn't see her.

"Alex!" Christopher called. When Alex found him, Christopher was leaning over a large garbage pail. "Come and take a look at this." Christopher held something up to the light. It looked like a small box dangling from a string.

Alex walked over to get a good look. Now he could tell it wasn't a box. It was square, green, and fuzzy. "Dice—er, die?" Alex said. He got too close to the fuzz. "Aachoo!"

Christopher took a picture of the fuzzy green thing. Then he photographed the mess in the kitchen. Alex didn't know what to do. The church ladies had all gone home, so there was nobody left to interview. He would have liked to run his ghost theory past Amanda and compare notes, but Amanda wasn't around.

Miss Jones drove the kids back to Puzzleworks. Korina stared out the car window the whole time. As the car turned onto the square, she finally spoke. "Miss Jones," Korina said, leaning forward, "were there any babies around the church today?"

Christopher turned to face Alex and Korina in the backseat of the station wagon. He raised his eyebrows at Korina. "Babies?" he asked.

"Or really little kids," Korina continued. "Did any kids crawl around the basement? Maybe some toddlers with long fingernails?"

"Hmmm," said Miss Jones. She glanced in the backseat. The car swerved to the right, causing Alex to bump into Korina. Miss Jones looked back at the road. "There was that little girl … Emma's granddaughter … Meg. But no babies."

As soon as Miss Jones pulled up to the curb in front of Puzzleworks, The Puzzle Club hopped out. It was dark inside and outside the shop. Tobias had put the "Closed" sign up. Alex pressed his face against the window and saw Tobias talking on the phone. Tobias waved the kids inside.

"Yes," Tobias was saying into the phone, "I'll be sure to tell them. You can count on the kids to do all they can. Tell the rest of the workers at the shelter that The Puzzle Club *and* The Jigsaw Kids are on the case."

Tobias hung up the phone and flipped on a light. "Well?" he asked. "Did you find the thief?"

Christopher shook his head. "What about The Jigsaw Kids, Tobias? Did you talk to Flash?" he asked.

"Did you talk to Kirk?" Korina asked.

"And Amanda?" Alex added.

Tobias sighed. "I did, but I'm not sure it did any good. I tracked The Jigsaw Kids down at the sheriff's office. Poor kids. They're determined to beat The Puzzle Club to the solution of this mystery."

"Did you tell Kirk that I was sorry, Tobias?" Korina asked.

"Yes, I did, Korina," Tobias said. "But I'm afraid he'll have to hear it from you before he believes it. Right now I'm not even sure those three realize how much they need good friends. They said they were too busy to make friends. They have a case to solve."

Tobias set a slice of pepperoni pizza in Sherlock's dinner dish. Sherlock started to eat. "So," Tobias said, "it looks like you Puzzle Club kids have your work cut out for you. Solving the church mystery—"

"And solving the mystery of how to make friends with our enemies," Korina finished.

"Who was on the phone?" Alex asked.

"That was the animal shelter," Tobias said. He closed the shades on his front windows and locked his cash register. "They're afraid the church sale will be canceled. If they don't get the money from the sale, they can't build the extra room to house unwanted animals."

"Well," Christopher said, yawning, "I need to develop some pictures. And Korina thinks she may have picked up a couple of clues at the church."

Tobias clicked off the light. The only glow in the dark room came through a crack in the window shade. "I think you three need to get a good night's sleep. You'll be fresher in the morning," he said.

The Puzzle Club agreed to meet early the next day. Alex went straight home and hit the hay early. That night he had at least a dozen dreams. In each one, he was chasing, or being chased by, a ghost thief. When he woke up and tried to remember his dreams, Alex was amazed. Not about the ghost thief of his dreams. He dreamed about ghosts all the time. What he couldn't get over was the fact that in every single dream, Amanda was with him.

7

Getting the Picture

As usual, Alex was the last one to arrive at Puzzle Club headquarters. He flung open the door. "Korina?" he called.

Korina sat in the middle of a great pile of giant coils and aluminum foil. Only her head stuck out. "I'm experimenting, Alex," she said. "I am working on a thief-catcher."

Alex looked at the big foil cage surrounding Korina. "Don't you think the thief will see this stuff a mile off?" he asked.

"This?" Korina asked, rattling the coils. "No, no, Alex. This is my model. Here's the real trap." Korina held out something that looked like a metal lunch box. "This is the thief-catcher."

Alex was afraid to touch the contraption. Wires ran in all directions. Two clothespins hung from wires on the sides. Little lights blinked on and off. Alex saw four batteries taped to another maze of wire. "That's going to catch the thief?" he asked.

"Oh, Alex," she said. "Sometimes you are so … proceed!"

Proceed? "Christopher," Alex shouted, "what does *proceed* mean?"

"Go!" Christopher yelled back.

Alex decoded. *Proceed—go. Go—* "I am not *slow,* Korina!"

"Alex," said Christopher, "come and take a look at these pictures." He was clothespinning an enlarged photo to a string that ran across the attic. Sherlock sat on top of the string, swaying slightly. Christopher had hung about two dozen pictures on the line.

The first picture was of The Jigsaw Kids. Alex couldn't take his eyes off Amanda. Her long black braid hung on her shoulder. He hadn't noticed how green her eyes were … or how big … or how … pretty.

"My favorite is the fourth photo," Korina said, still tinkering with her invention.

Alex couldn't help himself. He counted one, two, three, four. It was a picture of Hamlet, his two paws planted firmly on Alex's chest. Alex lay flat on the junkyard gravel. "You're pork, Korina," muttered Alex.

"*Braawk! Pork!*" squawked Sherlock.

"Alex," Christopher said. "Pork?"

"As in pork'n'*bean—mean*," Korina explained without turning to look at them. "Not bad, Alex."

"Come on, you two," Christopher said. "Alex, take a look at this one." He took one of his photos off the line. "You were right when you thought you saw something in the Puzzle Club secret chute, Alex. See?"

Alex could barely make out the inside of the Puzzle Club tunnel. The picture was dark. But right in the middle, there were the two red, beady eyes Alex had seen as he slid out to the street! It made him shiver. "I told you!" he said. "It *is* a ghost thief, just like Amanda said."

"Honestly, Alex," Korina said. "The way you two jump to conclusions! You were made for each other."

Alex started to answer, but Christopher pulled him to the other end of the photo line. "Tell me what you see here, Alex," he said.

The picture had been shot in the church basement. It was the big, green furry die. "Dice," Alex answered. "So what? We saw it when we checked the church yesterday."

"Die," Korina corrected. "It's *die* for one, *dice* for two."

"But do you remember where you saw it before?" Christopher asked.

Alex thought. Where had he seen that green, fuzzy … "I've got it! We saw it at Junkyard Jimmy's!" Alex said.

Christopher nodded. "Now, take a look at these," he invited.

Alex studied the photos as Christopher handed them to him. They were all taken at the junkyard. Christopher had taken shots of the red Volkswagen outside and inside. Alex remembered the honk they'd heard at the junkyard. Could that have been the thief? But why would he honk? Why would he give himself away?

"I was starting to form a theory about our thief," Christopher said. "Look closely, Alex. What do you see?"

Alex stared at the car seat, then at the floor of the car. What first looked like specks on the picture started to take shape. "Corn?" Alex said. "Is it Indian corn?"

"Bingo!" Christopher said.

"But who … what … why?" Alex said.

"That was the question," Korina said. "Now, put it together with my print analysis." Korina produced an aluminum tray, the kind Alex's mom had used to hold her paint roller when she'd painted the den. Four tiny handprints were imprinted in a white, hardened mixture in the tray.

"I made these prints from the flour and sugar in the church kitchen," Korina explained. "These prints are why I asked Miss Jones about a baby. You must admit they do look like a baby's hand-prints—a baby with long fingernails. Well, you can see that when we put together my print evidence and Christopher's photographic evidence—"

"And Alex's masked red-eyed monster, don't forget," Christopher broke in.

"Yes. Well, of course we then have our answer," Korina finished.

"Of course," Alex said. He didn't want to admit that he had no idea how they had put it together or what they got when they did.

"The thief-catcher is ready," Korina said. "Let's go set it up."

Tobias hung a "Be back in 20 minutes" sign on his front door and drove The Puzzle Club to Junkyard Jimmy's. "It's always so exciting when you get to the capture, isn't it?" Tobias said. "I only wish we'd been able to get hold of The Jigsaw Kids. I left messages for them to meet us at Sheriff Grimaldi's later though. I know you plan to share this victory with your friends."

Alex hid behind Tobias as they walked into the junkyard. Hamlet took an immediate liking to Tobias. So did Jimmy. Tobias and Jimmy chatted

54

while Alex watched Korina and Christopher set up the trap inside the red Volkswagen.

Korina set the box carefully on the front seat. Then Christopher dropped Indian corn in a trail leading to the Volkswagen. Korina was still hard at work inside the car, attaching wires and hooking things up. When she was done, Christopher poured a pile of corn inside the trap.

Korina stepped out of the car and closed the door gently, explaining her invention. "It is rather simple, really," she said. "I have made my reactor pressure sensitive. The moment weight is applied to the box floor, my wires signal the magnetic device. The levers stroke down, tightening the wires attached to the trap door. The door slides down, and our thief is trapped."

"In that box?" Alex asked. Alex wasn't sure what he'd thought Korina's box was supposed to do, but it wasn't this! What could possibly fit inside that box? And if he'd been right all along and they were looking for a ghost, then her box couldn't hold it.

Tobias said he had to get back to the store. Jimmy took Hamlet for another hamburger. Christopher, Korina, and Alex ducked behind an old trailer and waited.

The Puzzle Club waited and waited. Alex's legs got stiff. A cold wind began to blow. Alex wished he'd brought his gloves ... or stayed home. "Nobody's coming," he whispered.

"Shh-hh," Korina scolded.

It must have been the bad night's sleep the night before that made Alex doze off. He awoke to a loud *click, click.*

"We've got him!" Korina cried. She and Christopher charged the red Volkswagen.

Alex's leg had fallen asleep. He hobbled after Korina. He could see the car, but he couldn't see anybody inside. Korina's invention must have failed.

Korina and Christopher cupped their hands around their eyes and pressed their faces against the windshield for a better look. "He's so cute, Christopher," cooed Korina.

"Your thieving days are over," Christopher said to the thief in the car. The horn honked once, twice, three times.

"Who is it?" Alex asked, pushing his way in for a better look.

There, scurrying back and forth in Korina's box, was the masked bandit. Alex recognized those beady eyes, that black mask. The mysterious thief was none other than a pesky raccoon!

8

Unmasking the Thief

"This is the thief?" Alex asked, staring at the gray, furry raccoon.

"The evidence did compute, Alex," Korina said. "One, raccoons leave paw prints that look just like a baby's handprints—if the baby had long fingernails, that is. Two, the fuzzy green dice—one in the church, left by said raccoon, and one in the car. A matched set. Three, beady red eyes and a mask. Four, items stolen: nuts, raisins, and other foodstuff."

"And now we've caught him in the act—so there's no mistake," Christopher said. "Early this morning I told Tobias my suspicions. He reminded me of a raccoon that had broken into his store when he had the Curiosity Shop a few years back. With those hand-like paws, raccoons can take off window screens, honk horns, and open car doors.

Tobias said one even turned on his car radio once."

"So what do we do now?" Alex asked.

"I think it's time we paid a visit to the animal shelter," Christopher said. "We can tell them the good news that the church mystery is solved. The craft and bake sale can go on as planned. And the shelter should know what to do with our little friend here."

Junkyard Jimmy and Hamlet came strolling out of the shed. "I see you caught your thief," Jimmy said.

Hamlet jumped up on Alex and slobbered all over him. Alex pulled off his backpack and dug through his emergency stuff. He found his purple winter stocking cap, the one that covered his whole face, except for his eyes and nose. He pulled on the cap. It had the desired effect. Hamlet whimpered and hid behind his master.

Tobias and Sherlock were waiting for them when The Puzzle Club walked into the animal shelter. "Jimmy was kind enough to phone me from his junkyard and fill me in. Congratulations, Puzzle Club," Tobias said. He peered into the cage Christopher clutched in both hands. "So this is our thief, is it?"

Sherlock flew to the top of the cage. He bent his head to peek in at the raccoon. "*Squawk! Thief!*" said Sherlock.

A teenaged volunteer in a white lab coat joined them. Alex recognized the boy from the Easter adventure. "Sherlock, isn't it?" the boy said, pointing to the Puzzle Club mascot. "I still say we always have room for a talkative parakeet."

Sherlock flew to safety on Alex's shoulder and didn't say a word.

"We are hoping you will find room for this misguided raccoon," said Korina.

"The Puzzle Club has solved the church mystery," Tobias said. "Now the shelter can build that extra room."

The volunteer stared at the masked raccoon. "In that case," he said, "welcome aboard." He took the raccoon to a special cage in the back of the shelter. "I'll keep him in the pen until the wildlife director can take him to our animal refuge."

"I'm proud of the way you handled this case," said Tobias. "You've saved the lives of a lot of poor creatures here. Now let's go meet The Jigsaw Kids at Sheriff Grimaldi's office."

"Did you tell them we solved the case with my thief-catcher?" Korina asked.

Tobias looked from Korina to Christopher to Alex. "I want you to think about The Jigsaw Kids and how they must feel," he said. "Now, more than ever, you're going to need to show them real friendship."

"You mean you don't want us to rub it in that we were the detectives who solved the case," Alex said. "That's it, isn't it, Tobias?"

"That's part of it, Alex," Tobias said. "Part of friendship is trying to imagine what your friend must feel like. Then do to your friend what you would like him to do to you, if he were in your shoes."

Alex tried to imagine how he would have felt if The Jigsaw Kids had solved the mystery without The Puzzle Club. He knew how he'd feel—yucky. What would he want Amanda to do if she were the winner and he were the loser? He sure would not want her to brag about it.

"We get it, Tobias," Korina said.

"Yeah," Christopher said. "Let's go meet our new friends."

The Jigsaw Kids were waiting inside with Sheriff Grimaldi when The Puzzle Club arrived at his office. "What's this about, Tobias?" asked the sheriff. "Flash said you told them to meet you here. Is anything wrong?"

"No, no," said Tobias. He unbuttoned his jacket. "Everything's fine, Sheriff. I just ... we just ... wanted everybody together to share ... uh ... thanks for a job well done."

"What's he talking about, Sheriff?" Flash asked. Watson, the parrot, looked fast asleep on her shoulder.

Alex felt Sherlock's claws dig into his shoulder. "The case is solved!" Alex said. He smiled at Amanda. She'd been smiling since he had walked into the room, but now she looked shocked.

"What did you say?" Kirk asked. "Is this some kind of cola?"

Cola—Coke. Coke—joke. Alex decoded in his head. "It's no joke, Kirk," Alex said. "We have the thief captured and caged right now."

"But, like Tobias said," Christopher explained, "you Jigsaw Kids did a great job of detective work. Everybody shares in the victory. And the most important thing is that the church women can relax. The sale can go on. And the animal shelter will get the money it needs to build another room. So everybody's a winner!"

Flash, Kirk, and Amanda had moved closer together while Christopher was talking. "Are you sure you solved the case?" Amanda asked. "I thought we could try to investigate again. Alex and I could share notes. We could—"

"Who did you capture? What's your evidence?" asked Flash.

Christopher ran through his deductions step by step, ending with the scene in the junkyard. "And there, just as I'd suspected, was a pesky raccoon!" he announced.

"Did you say *raccoon*?" Kirk asked. "As in the nocturnal mammal?"

"We trapped him with my thief-catcher," Korina said. "I shall be happy to demonstrate it for you, Kirk. And I'm really sorry about what I said before. I would like us to be friends—"

"Wait just a minute," Flash said. "I'm not sure I buy all of this. Are you trying to tell me a raccoon was behind this whole operation?"

"Maybe we should keep investigating—together," Amanda suggested again. She smiled at Alex, and he felt his face grow warm.

"*Braawk! Together!*" said Sherlock.

"*Squawk! Thief!*" bellowed Watson, sending poor Sherlock full-speed out the door.

"Well, congratulations again, Puzzle Club," said Sheriff Grimaldi. He shook each of their hands. "I knew I could count on you to solve the case."

"And don't forget The Jigsaw Kids, Sheriff," said Tobias. "They worked very hard on this case."

Flash and Kirk moved toward the door, but

Amanda hung back. "Does this mean it's over?" Amanda asked.

"Now don't be poor sports, Jigsaw Kids," said Sheriff Grimaldi. "The Puzzle Club always gets their man—even when he's a raccoon!" The sheriff laughed so hard at his own joke that he started to cough.

"Where are you going, Flash?" Christopher asked. "Come by Puzzleworks later. You still haven't seen Puzzle Club headquarters."

"I need to buy film," Flash said. "We'll see you around." She stepped out the door and headed across the street.

"Infant," Kirk said.

Alex thought in Kirk Code. *Infant—baby. Baby—maybe.* Maybe they'll see us around?

Amanda sighed, then followed Kirk out the door.

The Puzzle Club walked in silence back to headquarters. This wasn't the way it was supposed to feel at the end of a case. Usually Alex was the first to celebrate when they cracked a big mystery. But he didn't feel like celebrating. For some reason, the sight of Amanda, her head hung low, kept popping into his mind.

Something was wrong. Very wrong. As Alex plodded up the stairs to headquarters, he had a weird feeling. Something told him this case wasn't closed.

9

The Agony of De-Feet

Friday morning Alex, Korina, and Christopher sat at Tobias' puzzle table gluing together an autumn puzzle. "I really appreciate your help," Tobias said. He squeezed clear glue from a big, blue bottle marked *Super Stick 'Em.* "I'll hang this puzzle in the front window as soon as it dries." He held up a section of the puzzle to admire it.

Suddenly the door flew open. Sherlock took off from Alex's shoulder. Tobias dropped the puzzle section, sending pieces sliding across the floor.

Alex jumped up to retrieve the pieces, tripped, and landed on his stomach. He opened his eyes to see somebody's pink tennis shoes inches from his nose.

"Alex, are you okay?" Amanda asked, helping him to his feet.

"*OKAY!*" screamed Watson, flapping down toward Alex like a vulture dive-bombing roadkill.

"I will be okay if you get this creature off me," Alex said.

Watson flapped to the ground, grabbed a puzzle piece, and dropped it in the right spot on the table. "*SQUAWK! ELEMENTARY!*" he said.

"Flash!" Christopher called, crossing the room to meet her. "You came. Great! I can show you my dark room and—"

"We're here on business," Flash interrupted.

"Motherly business," Kirk said.

Korina muttered as she decoded, "*Motherly—protective? Protective—detective!* You're here on detective business?"

Alex whipped out his notebook. "A new case? Already?"

"Not a *new* case," Flash said. "An *old* case."

"What do you mean?" Christopher asked.

"The church with the craft and bake sale, the one where Amanda's grandfather works," Flash said and paused to look from one baffled Puzzle Club member to the other, "has just been robbed—again. The church thief is still on the loose, Christopher. Looks like The Puzzle Club goofed!"

"Goofed?" Alex repeated the word.

"*SQUAWK! GOOFED!*" Watson flew circles around Alex.

"But ... but ... The Puzzle Club doesn't ... goof," Alex said.

"This is simply not possible," Korina said, shaking her head so her straight, black hair whipped back and forth.

"But our test ... Korina's trap ..." Christopher frowned and paced the floor of Puzzleworks.

Tobias stood in the middle of the two groups of kids. "That's not important now, Christopher. And everybody makes mistakes, Alex," Tobias said.

"I'll say," Kirk muttered.

Tobias put a hand on Christopher's shoulder. "What's important now is getting to the bottom of this mystery before it's too late," Tobias said. "The sale is tomorrow. You're going to have to work together and be friends. You need each other!"

"Don't you worry, Mr. Tobias," Flash said. "The Jigsaw Kids are on the case! In fact, we were never really off."

"We had better get to the church," Christopher said, pulling on his jacket.

"I'll pray that you get there in time," said Tobias as the kids raced out of Puzzleworks. "Remember—cooperate!"

Alex ran back inside to get his cape and Sherlock Holmes hat. When he got back outside, everybody but Amanda was gone.

"Come on, Alex," Amanda said. "We can compare notes on the way."

Amanda and Alex pedaled toward the church. "You know, Alex," Amanda said, "I think you were right all along. It *is* a ghost thief. We should have listened to you."

"You don't think I was jumping to conclusions?" Alex asked.

"Oh, no, Alex," Amanda said, staring at him and not even looking where she was biking. "You don't jump to conclusions, as far as I can see. You just figure things out before everybody else so it looks like you're jumping."

Alex liked the sound of that. Maybe Amanda was right. "You know, I kind of did think all along it was a ghost thief," he said. "I wrote that in my notebook." If he hadn't needed both hands to steer his bike, he would have showed her.

Amanda let go of her handlebars, but her bike kept right on course. She flipped open her notebook. "Yep. Right here. I wrote, 'Alex believes we have a ghost thief.' I'm really glad I get to tag along with you, Alex," Amanda said.

"Me too, Amanda," Alex said. And he meant it. Maybe Tobias was right about making friends with The Jigsaw Kids. Amanda was okay.

"*Braawk! Elementary, dear Watson! Elementary, dear Watson!*" This time it was Sherlock squawking and chasing the big, green parrot!

Alex and Amanda laughed as Watson flapped in circles to stay out of Sherlock's way. "Hey, Sherlock!" Alex hollered. "Be friends!"

Sherlock rode the rest of the way to the church on Alex's handlebars while Watson perched on Amanda's. Flash and Christopher already were interviewing the flustered Miss Jones when Alex and Amanda walked into the main basement room.

"So the money was here when you came in this morning, Miss Jones?" Flash asked.

"Yes, dear," said Miss Jones. "At about 10 o'clock, I added 10 one-dollar bills to our money box to make sure we'd have enough change for the sale tomorrow."

"Was anyone else here at the time?" Christopher asked. Alex moved closer so he could record all the answers. Amanda stuck with him.

"Mrs. Willakers was over there, finishing the wreaths." Miss Jones pointed a shaky finger toward one corner of the basement where a table covered with wreaths stood. "And, of course, Amanda and her grandfather were finishing mopping the floors. I don't remember anyone else."

"So the thief stole the money right from under your nose?" Korina asked.

"I guess so," said Miss Jones. "Along about noon, Mrs. Willakers made the final tally on the money. That's when we discovered the money box was empty."

Alex stepped between Flash and Christopher. "Miss Jones, what we've got here is a ghost thief," he announced.

Miss Jones gasped.

"Alex had it right all along!" Amanda said.

"But ... but," Miss Jones sputtered, "I thought you said it was a raccoon."

"The Puzzle Club were tune," Kirk said.

Miss Jones looked more confused than ever.

"*Tune—song. Song—wrong,*" Korina translated for Miss Jones.

It was too much for poor Miss Jones. "I'm afraid I just can't take any more," she said. "I'm going home for a nap. Unless you can find the real thief, we'll have to cancel the sale. I'm sorry." She pulled on her coat and trotted up the stairs.

"Way to go, Alex! Still jumping to conclusions," Korina said.

"You can call it jumping if you want to, Korina," Alex said, "but I knew all along it was a ghost thief." He nodded at Amanda, who nodded back.

Christopher was on his hands and knees, crawling across the floor. The phone in the kitchen rang. Christopher went to answer it and everyone trailed along. "Tobias? ... But how?" Christopher said. "Slow down ... When? ... Don't worry! We'll be right over!"

All the detectives stared at Christopher. His face had gone white as a ghost thief. "What's up?" Flash asked.

"It's Tobias," Christopher said, his forehead wrinkled in a frown. "He's been robbed!"

10

Sticking Together

"We'd better get to Puzzleworks!" Christopher said.

Alex looked around for Amanda, but she was nowhere in sight. By the time he got to the bikes, Flash and Kirk already were riding away. Amanda waved to Alex. "Alex, here!" She handed Alex his bike.

"Hey! What's going—" Flash yelled.

"Watch out!" screamed Kirk.

Alex looked up just in time to see Kirk and Flash topple over, bikes and all. They lay on the soft grass, still half on their bikes.

"Are you okay?" Christopher asked, pulling Flash's bike off of her. Her shoes stayed with the bike, stuck to the pedals!

Korina was trying to help Kirk stand up, but his shoes were stuck to his pedals too! "Let me untie your shoes," Korina said, trying to untie the laces. "How did this happen?"

"The solution is quite clear," Kirk said. "Someone has put glue on the pedals of our bikes to hamper this investigation."

Amanda had stopped just in time. "Looks like my pedals have been glued too," she said.

Alex checked his bike. "Mine are okay," he said.

"Mine too," said Christopher.

Korina ran over and checked her bike. "No glue here," she said.

Flash stood up, shoeless, and examined her bike. "Now isn't that a coincidence," she said. "Jigsaw bikes are glued. Puzzle Club bikes are not."

"Flash," Christopher said, "you don't think we had anything to do with this!"

"Highly yummy if you ask me," Kirk said, tugging his shoes from the pedals.

Korina thought out loud, "*Yummy—delicious. Delicious—suspicious?* Why, we would never—"

"Shouldn't we get over to Puzzleworks?" Amanda suggested. "Alex, could I ride with you on your bike?"

"Good idea," Christopher said. "Flash, you can ride with me. Kirk can go with Korina."

Alex almost tipped his bike over twice on the ride to Tobias' store. He wasn't used to riding double. Every time Amanda turned back and smiled at him, he almost lost his balance. Sherlock and Watson bailed out and hitched a ride with Korina and Kirk.

"I didn't mean for you to leave the church," Tobias said as everyone walked into Puzzleworks. "I just thought you'd want to know in case it's the same thief."

"What did the ghost thief take?" Alex asked.

Tobias looked puzzled. "Ghost thief? But ... I ... er ... glue."

"Glue?" Christopher repeated.

Alex shot a glance toward the puzzle table. The big blue bottle of *Super Stick 'Em* was gone! "The glue we were using to put together the puzzle?" Alex asked.

"One mystery solved," Flash said, her hands on her hips. "Now we know where *somebody* got the glue for our bikes so The Jigsaw Kids wouldn't solve the case first."

"No, Flash," Tobias said gently. "I've been friends with The Puzzle Club for a long time. They'd never do that. I just wish you kids would try to be friends. Then maybe you could solve this case and save those poor animals at the shelter."

"Mr. Tobias," Amanda said, "what did you mean about saving the animals at the shelter?"

"That's why the church is having the sale, Amanda," Tobias said. "The money goes toward building another room at the shelter. If they can't build, they'll have to get rid of some of the animals."

"Get rid of them?" Amanda looked shocked. "Mr. Tobias, would you give us a ride back to the church?"

Tobias was only too willing to drive everyone to the church in his van. Alex sat next to Amanda, who didn't say a word the whole way. She just scribbled in her notebook.

Tobias wheeled around a corner and pulled to a stop in front of the church. Everybody piled out of the van and ran to the basement. Korina and Kirk dusted the money box for fingerprints. Christopher and Flash snapped pictures of the scene.

Alex was trying to peer over Korina at the money box when he felt a tap on his shoulder. "Amanda!" Alex said, "I wondered where you were."

"Let's search for the money," she said. "We could start over there—by the wreaths." When Alex hesitated, Amanda pleaded. "Maybe we missed something."

Alex shrugged. He was pretty sure that by now the ghost had disappeared with the money. But it wouldn't hurt to go along with Amanda.

"You look under here," Amanda said, pointing to a long table of wreaths. "I'll check through the wreaths."

Alex thumbed through a big box of supplies under the table, but he knew he wouldn't find anything. Sherlock swooped into the box and came up with a piece of paper sticking to his beak.

"What's this?" Alex asked, taking the paper from Sherlock.

"Read it, Alex," Amanda said, unfolding the note in his hands.

Alex read the shaky red writing—letters that looked as if a ghost had written them. For a minute Alex wondered if they had been written in blood, but it was only red ink. "Look under the garbage bag under the kitchen sink.—Ghost Thief."

"I was right!" Alex said. "This proves it."

Amanda whispered to Alex, "Go ahead, Alex! Go look under the sink like the ghost said."

Alex raced to the kitchen. "Step aside, please," he told Korina and Kirk.

"Alex," Korina said, "we are in the middle of scientific investigations. You might at least—"

"I know where the money is!" Alex announced.

Christopher, Tobias, and Flash came running into the kitchen. "Alex," Tobias said, "did you find the money?"

"I believe your answer is right here!" Alex said. Then, as dramatically as he could, he reached under the sink and pulled out the trash can. Alex stuck his hand down inside the slimy trash and felt for the money. He touched banana peels, yucky coffee grounds, small bones, a milk carton, but no money.

Alex reached deeper, his whole arm sinking into the slimy mess. It smelled like rotten pumpkins. "P.U!" Alex said.

Sherlock and Watson flew in at the same time and rested on the trash can. "*Braawk! P.U.!*" said Sherlock.

"*SQUAWK! P.U.!*" said Watson, actually agreeing with Sherlock.

"Nice going, Alex," Korina said. "Now may we get back to our investigation?"

Amanda knelt down next to Alex and whispered in his ear, "Alex, look *under* the garbage bag."

Alex pulled his arm out of the garbage and shook off the coffee grounds that had stuck to his sleeve. He grabbed the garbage bag and lifted it out of the trash can. There, on the bottom of the can, was a pile of money! "It's here!" shouted Alex. "I knew the ghost thief wouldn't lie!"

Tobias reached down and collected the money. "But, Alex, how did you know where to look?" he asked.

"He's just a great detective," Amanda suggested.

"The ghost thief must have known I'd find him sooner or later," Alex said. "He left me this note telling me where to find the money."

Christopher took the note and studied it. "I had a pretty good idea who your ghost thief was, Alex. But now I'm sure," Christopher said.

"What do you mean?" Alex asked.

"Don't you recognize this note paper, Alex?" Christopher asked.

Alex took the note back. It looked a lot like the paper in his detective's notebook—except for the lines. This one didn't have any lines. That was it—no lines! "Amanda?" he guessed.

Flash grabbed Amanda's pink notebook and flipped it open. She pointed to frayed paper at the top of the spiral. "Amanda, there's a page missing. You always save all your detective notes." Flash glared at Amanda. "*You* wrote that note!"

"And *you* stole that money! Tardier!" Kirk screamed at Amanda.

Alex figured that one out easily. *Tardier—later. Later—traitor!* "But, Amanda," he said, "you're the ghost thief?"

"She wasn't. Not all along," Christopher explained. "We had the right thief. The raccoon stole everything—except for the money and the glue."

"*You* glued our bikes!" Kirk said, as if that piece of the puzzle had just clicked in. "How could you?"

Amanda's whole body shook as tears poured down her cheeks. Tobias handed her a handkerchief. "Now, now, Amanda," he said. "Tell us all about it, won't you? You'll feel better."

Amanda wiped her eyes. "It's just … I didn't want the mystery to end. I liked having Alex as a friend. I was afraid if the mystery got solved …" Amanda hid her face. "If it was solved, you guys would stop being our friends. But now I've ruined everything. Now I've even lost my old friends."

Flash and Kirk turned their backs on Amanda and started toward the door.

"Wait!" Alex said. Flash and Kirk stopped, but they didn't turn around. "Please, you can't just stop being friends because someone messes up.

If The Puzzle Club worked that way, Korina and Christopher would never be my friends!"

"Please come back," Christopher said. "Alex is right. It's not always easy being friends. But real friends forgive each other."

"Tobias taught us a lot about friendship," Korina said. "Tell them that verse about friendship, Tobias."

Tobias quoted from the gospel of Matthew again: "Love your enemies ... If you love those who love you, what reward will you get?"

"Jesus is our best Friend," Alex said. "He loves us so much that He gave His life for us. He helps us to be friends with each other and to treat our friends like He treats us. You don't have to give up old friends when you get new ones. Jesus will help us work on friendship like He helps us work on mysteries."

Flash turned around. "I guess I'm not always such a great friend myself," she said.

"I admit, I do see the logic," Kirk said. "And we scientists are not always easy to get along with."

Amanda sniffed softly, then peered up at her friends. "I'm really sorry about gluing your bikes," she said. "All I could think about was making Alex the hero. But I love being part of The Jigsaw Kids. Can I still be one?"

Flash and Kirk grinned at each other, then at Amanda. "Put her there, friend," Flash said, holding out her hand.

Amanda ran over and shook Flash's hand, then Kirk's. Christopher was next. "Great. Friends?" he said, sticking out his hand. Everybody shook everybody else's hand—except Korina and Kirk.

"Korina? Kirk?" Tobias pleaded.

Korina made the first move and held out her hand. "What do you say, Kirk?" she asked.

"Finish," Kirk said.

"Finish?" Korina repeated, jerking back her hand. "Well, if you want to finish, then—"

"*SQUAWK!*" said Watson, coming to a landing right on top of Korina's head. "*FINISH!*"

"Korina," Alex said, "*Finish—End!*"

Sherlock zoomed in and perched on top of Kirk's head. "*Braawk! End—Friend!*"

Korina and Kirk burst out laughing and joined hands in a firm handshake. "Brilliant deduction, Sherlock," Korina admitted.

"*Braawk!*" Sherlock answered. "*Elementary, dear Watson!*"